D0589981

This Walker book belongs to:

....

....

....

For Josie and Oliver

First published 1995 by Walker Books Ltd
87 Vauxhall Walk, London SE11 5HJ

This edition published 2012

2 4 6 8 10 9 7 5 3 1

© 1995 Lucy Cousins

Lucy Cousins font © 1995 Lucy Cousins

The right of Lucy Cousins to be identified as author/illustrator of the work
has been asserted by her in accordance with the Copyright, Designs and Patents Act 1988

Printed in China

British Library Cataloguing in Publication Data:
a catalogue record for this book is available from the British Library.

ISBN 978-1-4063-3579-8

www.walker.co.uk

WALKER BOOKS
AND SUBSIDIARIES

LONDON • BOSTON • SYDNEY • AUCKLAND

Za-Za's
Baby Brother

Lucy Cousins

My mum is going to have a baby.

She has a big fat tummy. There's not much room for a cuddle.

Granny came to
look after me.

Dad took mum to the hospital.

When the baby was born we went to see Mum.

All my uncles and aunts came to see the baby.

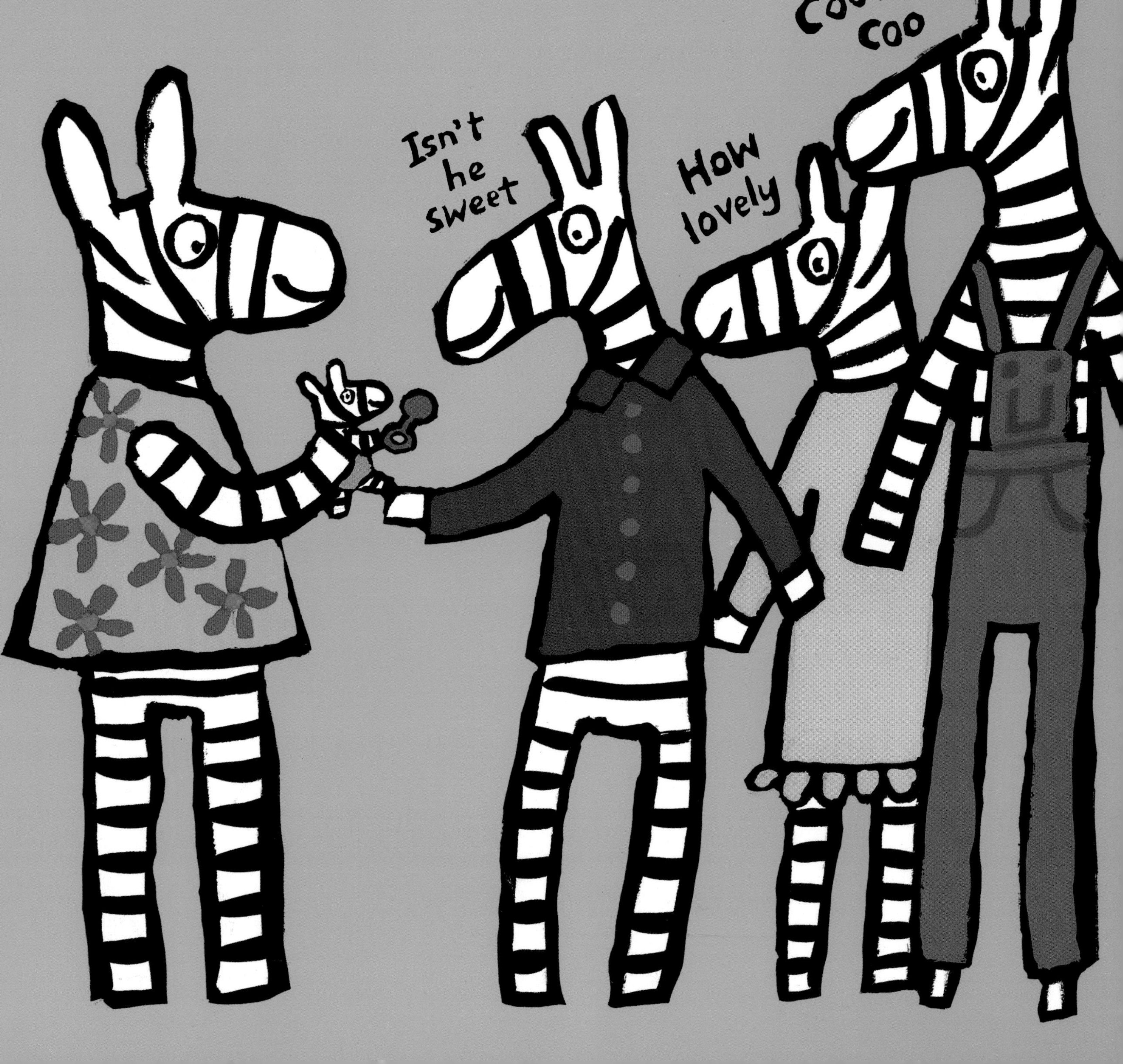

what a
good
boy

ooh he's
gorgeous

I played on
my own.

Dad was always busy.

Mum was always busy.

"Dad, will you read me a story?"
"Not now, Za-za.
We're going shopping soon."

"Sorry, Za-za, baby's hungry and we have to go home."

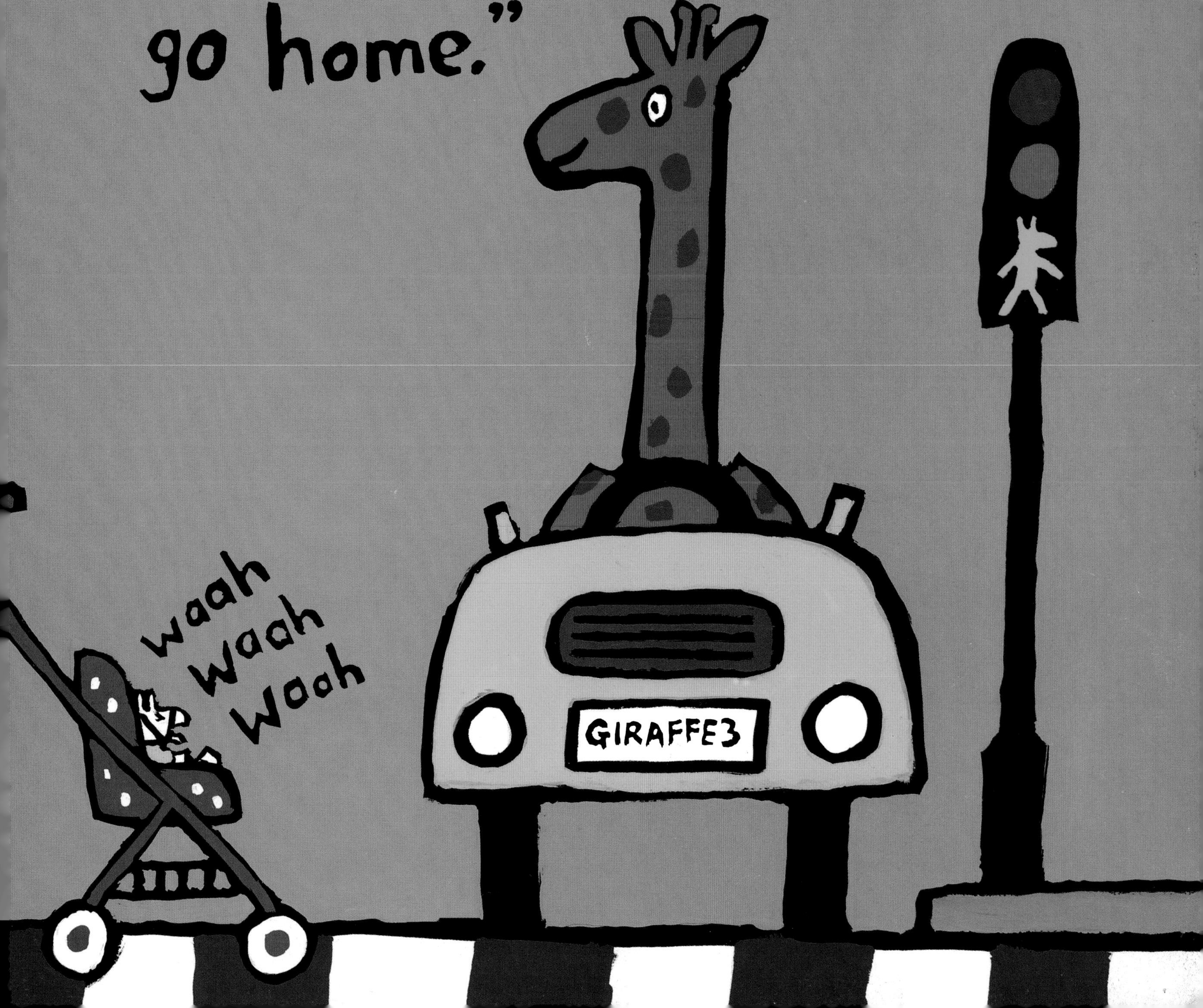

"Can I have **my** tea soon?"

"Yes, Za-za."

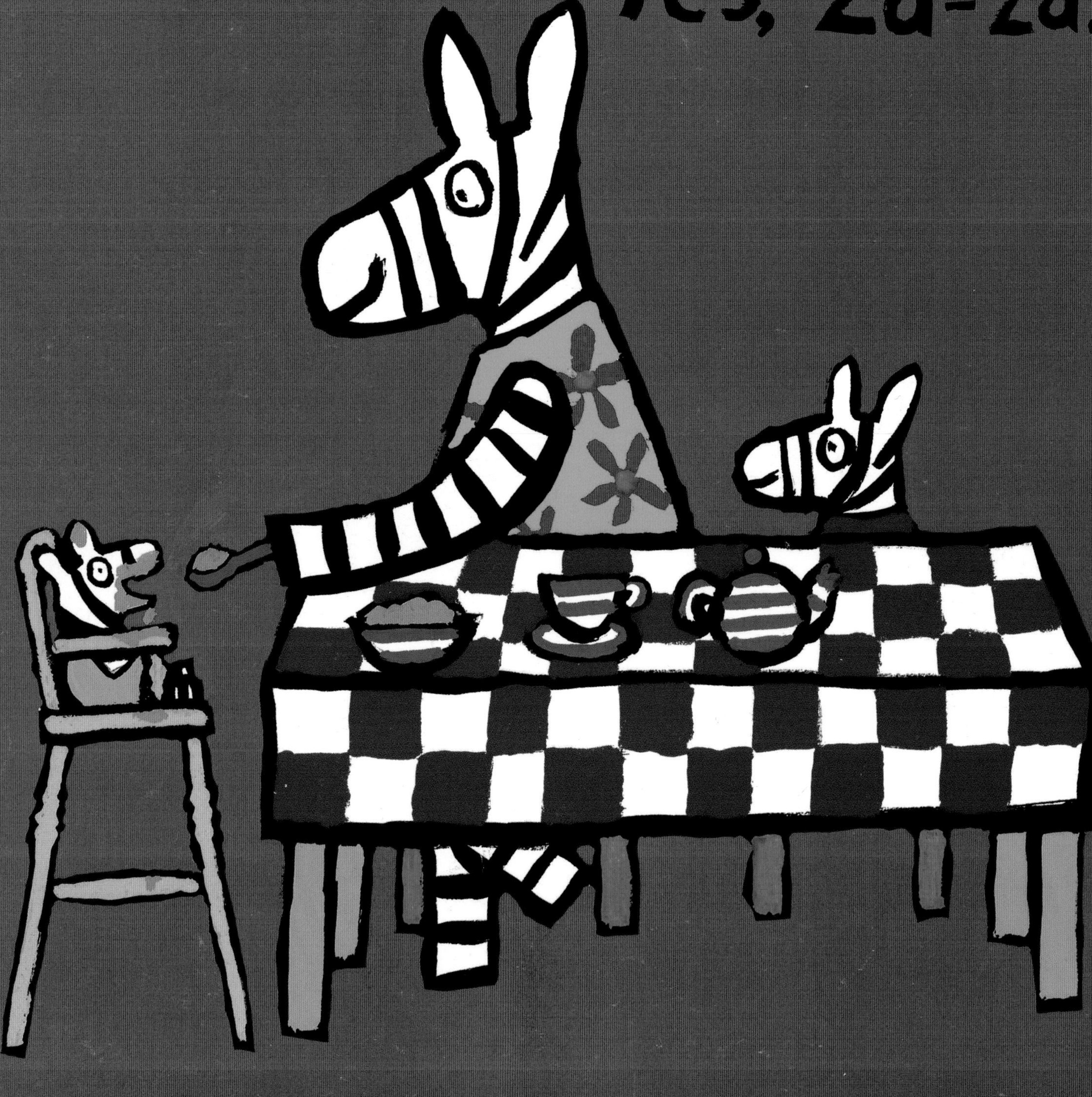

So I cuddled the baby...

and I pushed him...

and I
built him
a tower.

He was nice.
It was fun.

When the baby got tired Mum put him to bed.

Then I got my
cuddle...

and a bedtime story.

Lucy Cousins

is the multi award winning creator of much-loved character Maisy.
She has written and illustrated over 100 books and has sold
over 25 million copies worldwide.

978-1-4063-2872-1

978-1-4063-0156-4

978-1-4063-3838-6

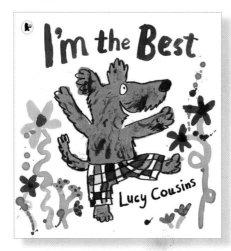

978-1-4063-2965-0

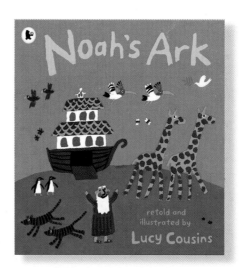

978-0-7445-9972-5

Available from all good booksellers

www.walker.co.uk